Curious George®

Race Day

Adaptation by Samantha McFerrin
Based on the TV series teleplay
written by John Loy

Houghton Mifflin Harcourt Publishing Company
Boston New York

For information about permission to reproduce selections from this book, write to trade.permissions@hmhco.com or to Permissions, Houghton Mifflin Harcourt Publishing Company, 3 Park Avenue, 19th Floor, New York, New York 10016.

Library of Congress Cataloging-in-Publication Data is on file.

ISBN: 978-0-547-41724-0 paper-over-board
ISBN: 978-0-547-39361-2 paperback

Design by Afsoon Razavi

www.hmhco.com

Printed in China
SCP 10 9 8 7 6
4500592000

Today, George was helping Professor
Wiseman train for a race.
George had never coached anyone.
It seemed fun and easy.

George started running.
"Wait for me!" said the professor.
She tried to follow George.

But very soon the professor said,
"I'm tired! Can we stop now?"
George was puzzled.
They had barely begun.

George returned home.
The man with the yellow hat
told him not to give up.
He gave George a fitness video.

George watched the video.
He took many notes.
He was ready to coach
Professor Wiseman!

The next day
George used his notes.
First, he and the professor stretched.
Then they ran at a steady pace.

When the professor got thirsty,
George gave her some water.
So far so good!

But Professor Wiseman thought
running was boring.
"I should get back to the museum,"
she said.
George did not understand.
Running was so much fun.
He was curious.
Could he make running fun for
the professor?

The next day, they ran to the Ferris wheel.
"The museum looks so small from up here," said the professor.

Then they ran to more of his
favorite places.
They ran to the puppet show and
to the zoo to see the elephants.

They even ran with balloons!

One day, the professor outran
George.
She was ready for the race!

On race day, George and the man went
to the park. There were so many people
there!

"Runners, take your marks!"
The whistle blew, and the runners took off.
George watched the professor as she ran.
It looked like she was having fun!

George wanted to see
the professor cross the finish line.

Suddenly she
stopped running!
George was confused.

Then the professor surprised George. "Will you finish the race with me?" she asked.

George and Professor Wiseman
ran together across the finish line.
She received a medal for finishing
the race.

The professor thanked George for
making exercise fun.
She had another surprise for George.
She wanted him to have her medal!

Having Fun Getting Fit!

In the story, George shows Professor Wiseman that running can be fun. Here's a game to get you jumping like a monkey—you won't even know you're exercising!

HOPSCOTCH

1. Use chalk or masking tape to create a diagram with eight sections. Each player has a marker, such as a stone or button.

2. The first player tosses her marker into the first square. She hops over square one to square two, then continues hopping to square eight and back again. She pauses in square two to pick up her marker, hops in square one, and hops out.

3. All hopping is done on one foot unless two squares are side by side.

4. The rest of the players take their turn, and then everyone continues by tossing his marker into square two.

5. A player is out if he misses a square, steps on a line, puts a foot down, or hops or lands in a square where there is a marker.

Everyday Ways to Stay Healthy!

When you exercise, you work and play hard! But did you know that staying fit is also as easy as closing your eyes?

Exercising makes you tired — **Get plenty of sleep!**
Be sure to recharge your body by sleeping at least eight hours a night.

Exercising makes you sweat — **Drink water before, during, and after!**
You can't play your best if you're thirsty.

Exercising uses energy — **Eat nutritious foods!**
You've heard about superheroes, but have you heard about superfoods? They are foods that pack a nutritious punch, such as avocados, blueberries, fish, sweet potatoes, beans, and oats. They taste good, too.

FLEX A LOUDER MUSCLE!

People can exercise anything from their legs to their arms to their neck to their fingers. Some people, such as singers or public speakers, even exercise their voice.

Try these simple vocal warm-up exercises and strengthen your voice, too!

1. Relax your face and jaw.
2. Stick out your tongue in all directions.
3. Make funny faces. Try to use all of the muscles in your face.
4. Make silly noises while shaking out your body or jumping up and down.
5. Yawn a few times.
6. Hum for ten seconds to get your lips and nose tingling.
7. Flap your lips making a "brr" sound.
8. Say "ahh" and let your voice rise and fall.
9. Sing or hum any song that makes you happy.

GRAYSLAKE AREA PUBLIC LIBRARY
100 Library Lane
Grayslake, IL 60030